Art Activities for Little Learners

15 Easy & Delightful Projects Using Everyday Materials

by Christy Hale

New York • Toronto • London • Auckland • Sydney
Mexico City • New Delhi • Hong Kong • Buenos Aires

Teaching *Resources*

For my friends at Sunflower daycare
and Brooklyn Friends preschool—C.H.

Cover, interior design, and illustration by Christy Hale

ISBN: 0-439-43464-5
Copyright © 2004 by Christy Hale
Published by Scholastic Inc.
All rights reserved.
Printed in the U.S.A.

2   3   4   5   6   7   8   9   10   40   11   10   09   08   07   06   05   04

Contents

Welcome to
Art Activities for Little Learners!

In these pages, you'll find adorable art projects just right for little hands! As you know, art is an important aspect of developing cognitive, emotional, and problem-solving skills. The early childhood learning environment is equipped with lots of art materials to encourage imagination and socialization. As a teacher, you set the stage for children's development by allowing them ample time for experiments and exploration, providing them with opportunities for involvement, and by planning for variety in their materials and activities. Along the way, you help them by extending their ideas, engaging others, and encouraging cooperation!

Manipulative play allows children to learn about materials and substances while developing fine motor skills and hand-eye coordination. Children can explore, experiment, and discover through their senses of touch and sight. The projects in this book are designed to provide varied art experiences (such as painting, collage, 3-D construction, printmaking, weaving, and paper folding), and cover many early childhood themes (such as all about me, family, home, autumn leaves, harvest, holiday giving, weather, Chinese New Year, transportation, Valentine's Day, spring, ocean life, and butterflies). For each project, you'll find a materials list, easy step-by-step instructions, and related books to help you kick off or extend the topic. And, an eight-page color insert lets you see each completed project.

Enjoy!

Materials

The projects are designed to use inexpensive, readily accessible materials. Many projects call for recycled materials. You might post a sign on your classroom door or send letters home (see page 61) asking for:

- Cardboard egg and milk cartons
- Shoe, tea, and cereal boxes
- Cardboard pieces
- Fabric scraps
- Paper grocery bags
- Cornhusks (saved and dried after shucking)
- Plastic bags
- String
- Cotton balls or jewelry box liners
- Lunch bags
- Used, sterilized toothbrushes
- Business envelopes with patterned linings
- Used manila folders
- Yogurt lids
- Plastic bottle caps
- Aluminum foil
- Clear, plastic food containers

Helpful Hints

- Provide each work area with plenty of moist towelettes when children are busy with messy projects, so they can clean their hands as they work.

- Gluing can be a messy job! Consider putting glue on a paper plate and providing cotton swabs for glue application.

- Enlist family volunteers to work with children individually or in small groups on more involved projects. Volunteers can also help you with project setup.

Movable Me

Children explore a favorite subject (themselves!) to create a movable twin.

Materials

DAY ONE

FOR EACH GROUP:
- Newspaper (to cover tables)
- Tempera paint to mix different skin tones (brown, black, white, orange, red, and yellow)
- Paintbrushes
- Shallow trays for mixing paints
- Tagboard (or recycled manila folders) for hand- and footprints, one per child

FOR EACH CHILD:
- Small paper plate
- 1 neck pattern and 2 each of arm and leg patterns (pages 10–11), copied onto heavy paper and cut out

DAY TWO

FOR EACH GROUP:
- Yarn for hair (black, brown, red, orange, and yellow)
- Pipe cleaners in varying lengths for eyebrows and mouths (black, brown, orange, yellow, red, and pink)
- Shirt and shorts templates (from the previous day's copies of pages 10–11), enough for each child
- Assortment of colored felt (precut to fit the shirt and shorts templates)
- Assortment of colored buttons and/or wiggle eyes
- Scissors
- Glue
- Hole punch
- 11 brads for each movable creation (or stapler)

DAY ONE

1 Discuss with children how they look the same as their friends, and how they are unique. Describe how we all have different skin tone, eye, and hair color. You might make a chart showing how many children in the class have blue, green, hazel, black, or brown eyes.

2 Divide the class into small groups. Cover each table with newspaper. Provide each group with tempera, paintbrushes, containers or shallow trays for mixing paints, and tagboard. Distribute a small paper plate, a neck pattern, and arm and leg patterns to each child. Label the backs of the pattern pieces with children's names.

3 Show children how to mix paint colors in the trays to match their skin tones. Add small amounts of paint when mixing to match. Begin with a light color; add darker colors a little bit at a time.

4 When children have mixed the desired skin color, have them pair up with a partner. Tell them to paint their partner's hands (the palm side) with his or her skin color, including the fingers. Children print each hand on the tagboard (allow enough tagboard for reprints). Label the prints with children's names.

5 Have children remove socks and shoes. Then, they paint their partner's feet with his or her skin color, and help him or her to step (carefully) onto tagboard to make a footprint of each foot (allow enough tagboard for reprints). Children can clean their feet with moist towelettes. Label the prints with children's names.

6 Invite each child to use his or her specially mixed skin color to paint the paper plate and the neck, arm, and leg patterns. Allow everything to dry on a flat surface.

DAY TWO

1 Provide each group with yarn, pipe cleaners, shirt and shorts templates, felt pieces, buttons and/or wiggle eyes, scissors, and glue. Provide children with their painted and dried pieces: hand- and footprints, painted paper plate, neck, arms, and legs.

2 Show children how they can cut and glue down yarn for hair on the upper portion of the paper plate. Then show them the selection of colored buttons and/or wiggle eyes. Demonstrate positioning and gluing eyes on the painted paper plate.

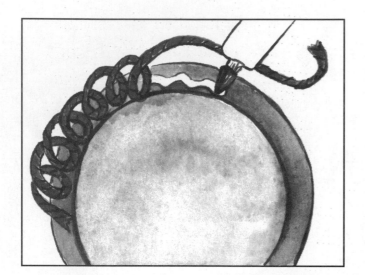 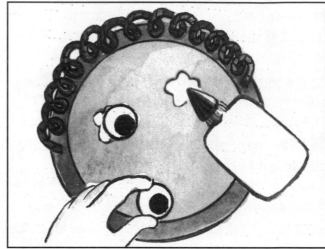

3 Show children how to glue pipe cleaners to make eyebrows and mouths. Encourage them to bend the pipe cleaners to show different expressions!

4 Distribute shirt and shorts templates and have children choose felt pieces to match. Demonstrate gluing the fabric to the tagboard templates. Allow everything to dry.

5 Have children cut out their hand- and footprints.

6 Have an adult work individually with children to help assemble the pieces, poking holes and inserting brads between:
• Head base and the top center of neck
• Neck base and the center neckline of shirt
• Each sleeve and top of arm
• Wrist of each arm- and handprint
• Center of shirt base and top center of shorts
• Each shorts leg
• Ankle of each leg and footprint
(See photo on page 6.)

NOTE: As an alternate, simpler approach, staple the pieces together.

7 Allow children to play with their "Movable Me" creations, then display them on a wall or bulletin board!

BOOK LINKS

I Like Being Me: Poems for Children, About Feeling Special, Appreciating Others, and Getting Along
by Judy Lalli
(Free Spirit Publishing, 1997)
Simple, memorable rhyming poems explore themes such as being kind, solving problems, learning from mistakes, being a friend, and more.

It's Okay to Be Different
by Todd Parr
(Little Brown & Co, 2001)
All kids will feel included in this simple, playful celebration of diversity.

I Like Me!
by Nancy L. Carlson
(Pearson, 1990)
Simple text teaches little ones to like themselves. The main character is one very upbeat pig!

Movable Me Patterns

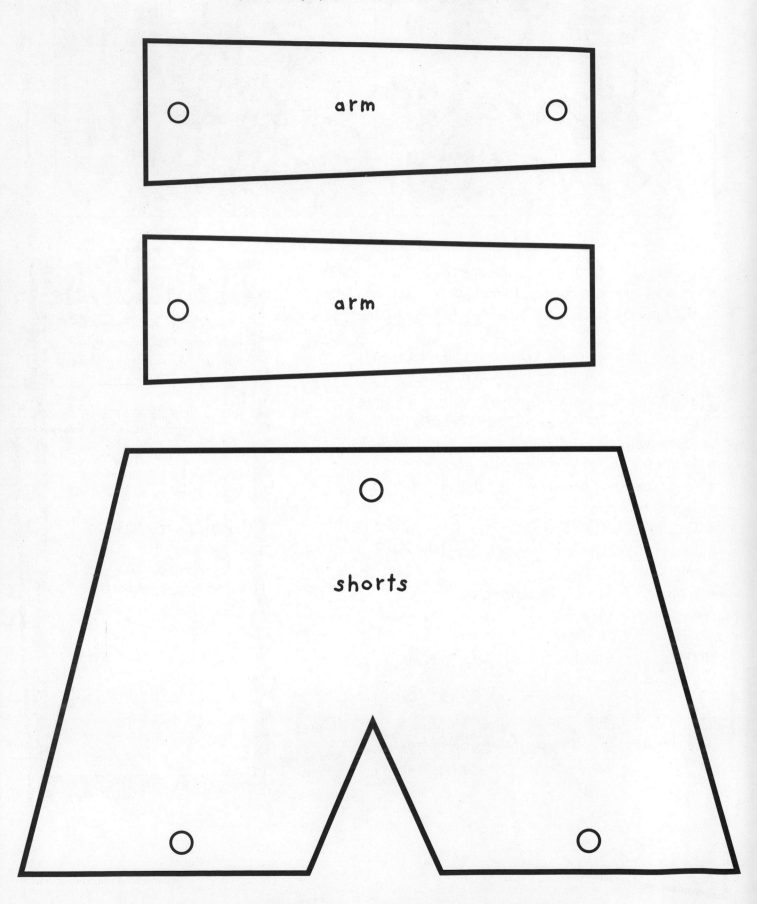

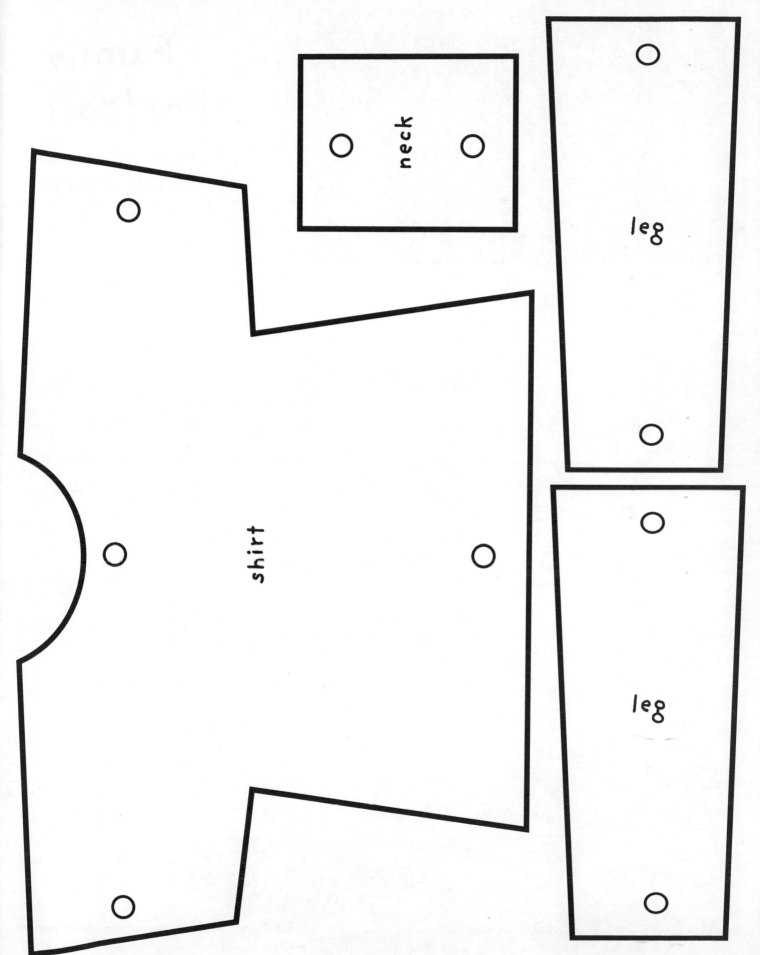

neck

leg

leg

shirt

Family Portrait

Children move beyond self-exploration to study their family.

Materials

- 11" x 14" sheet of cardboard, one per child
- Corrugated cardboard (to precut heads, arms, legs, and torsos; for size guide, see pages 14–15)
- Precut fabric scraps in the shapes and sizes of torsos, pants legs, and sleeves
- Wiggle eyes
- Yarn
- Pipe cleaners precut in different lengths
- Scissors
- Glue

1 What is a family? Discuss with children the many people who might make up a family.

2 Divide the class into groups. Provide each table with cardboard backings, precut corrugated cardboard body parts and patterned fabric scraps, wiggle eyes, yarn, pipe cleaners, scissors, and glue.

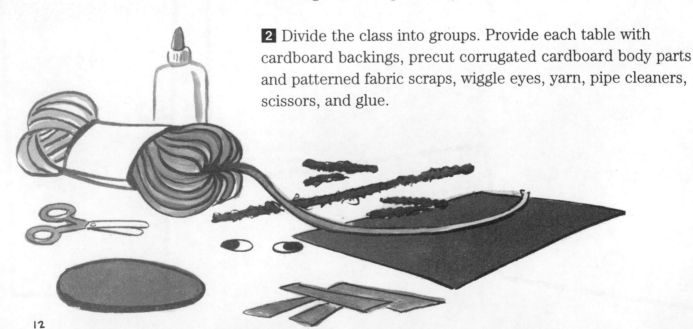

3 Show children how to combine the cardboard shapes to create a person. Encourage children to create large and small people to correspond to the members of their family.

4 Have children arrange their families on the backings and glue in place.

5 Demonstrate how to clothe the torsos, legs, and arms with the fabric scraps. Have children glue the fabric to the cardboard body parts.

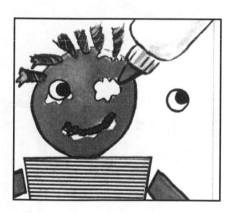

6 Show children how to make hair using yarn or pipe cleaners. Have them glue the hair in place.

7 Demonstrate how to glue down wiggle eyes and pipe cleaner mouths to show facial expressions.

8 Allow all elements to dry thoroughly.

9 Display the family portraits and have children introduce their families to the group!

BOOK LINKS

All Families Are Different
by Sol Gordon
(Prometheus Books, 2000)
This book introduces some simple but important ideas about what makes a family.

The Kissing Hand
by Audrey Penn
(Child Welfare League of America, 1993)
When Chester the raccoon is reluctant to go to kindergarten for the first time, his mother teaches him a secret way to carry her love with him.

Family Portrait Patterns

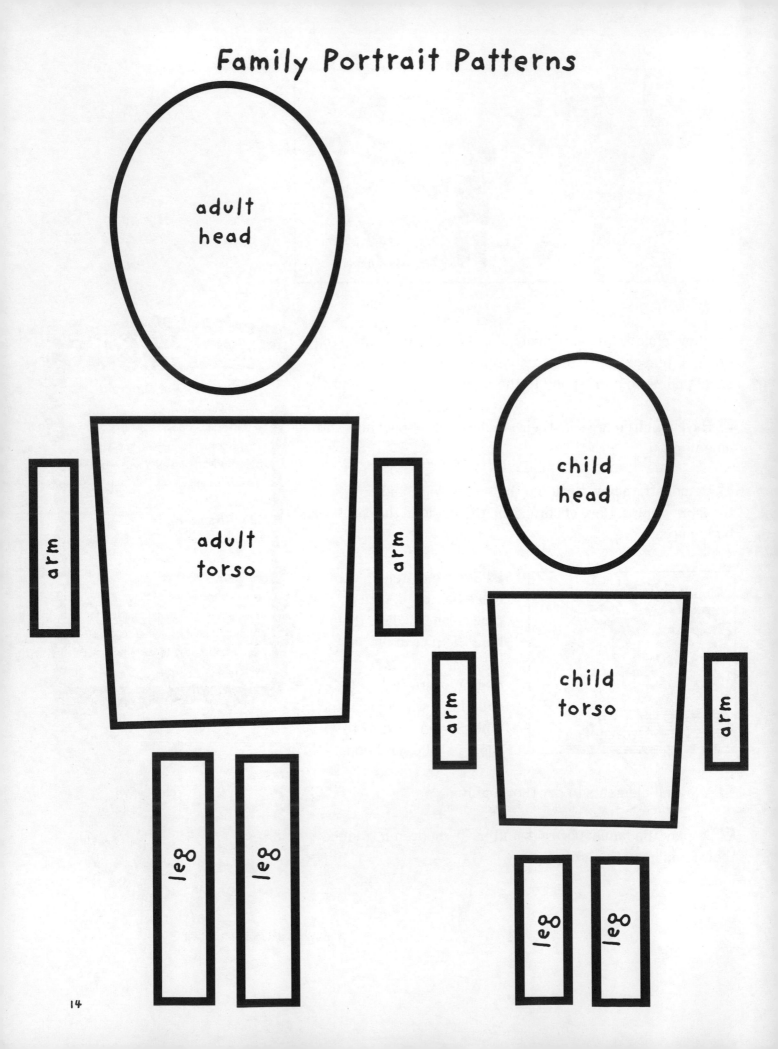

Family Portrait Patterns

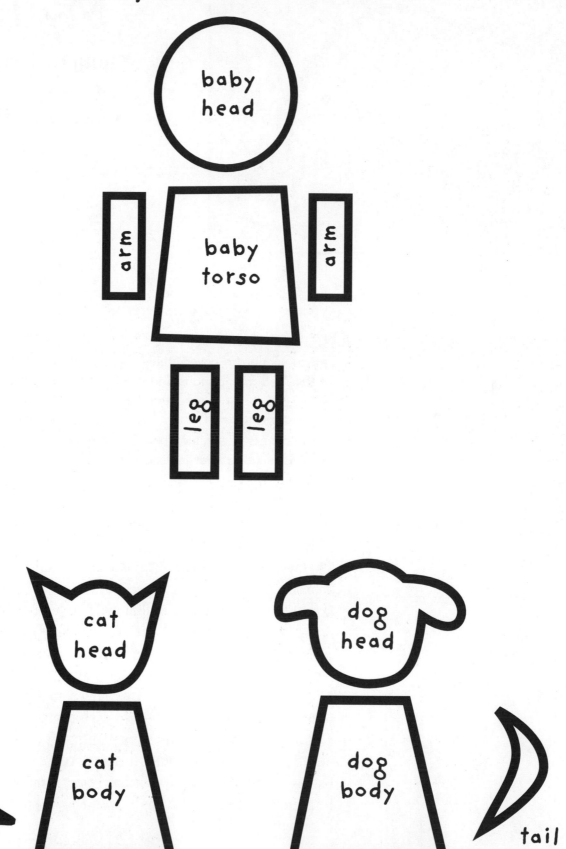

My Home

Children work in three dimensions to create a model of their home.

Materials

- Newspaper (to cover tables)
- Recycled milk cartons and cereal and shoe boxes
- Tempera paint in assorted colors
- Paintbrushes
- Containers or shallow trays for paints
- Construction paper in assorted colors
- Glue
- Scissors

DAY ONE

1 Have a discussion about homes. Ask children each to describe the building in which they live. Is the building tall? Long? What color is the building? How many windows does it have? What color is the roof? (Be aware of different living situations and avoid comparison of size and standard of living.)

2 Divide the class into groups. Cover each table with newspaper. Provide each group with tempera, paintbrushes, containers or shallow trays for paints, recycled milk cartons and boxes. After each child has selected a carton or box to use as the home, have him or her select a color of tempera to paint it. Children can then paint the boxes and leave overnight to dry.

DAY TWO

1 Provide each group with an assortment of colored construction paper, glue, and scissors.

2 Have children select a color of construction paper for the roof. Help them fold the paper in half lengthwise, try out the roof on top of the home, and trim excess length.

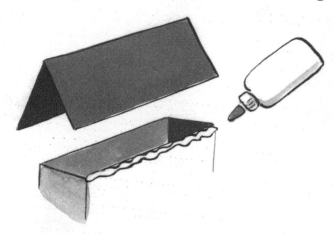

3 Demonstrate how to attach the roof to the base of the home. Glue along the top edges of the home, position the roof in place, and hold until glue sets.

4 Provide children with construction paper scraps for cutting out windows, doors, stairs, and any other details. Point out the different shapes children can use: square, rectangle, circle, and so on.

5 Help children glue these pieces in place and leave to dry.

6 Organize the many homes to create a classroom neighborhood. Later, you might also have children practice reading or writing their address information at the writing center.

Autumn Tree Prints

Children will enjoy creating fall foliage with this easy printmaking activity.

Materials

- Newspaper (to cover tables)
- 12" x 18" green construction paper, one sheet per child
- Cornhusks (ask families to put aside husks to dry at home after shucking), one per child
- Paintbrushes
- Plastic bags (recycled shopping bags), one per child
- Tempera paints (brown, red, orange, and yellow)
- Shallow containers for each color of tempera paint

1 Divide the class into groups. Cover work surfaces with newspaper. Provide each group with construction paper, cornhusks, paintbrushes, plastic bags, and tempera paints in shallow containers.

2 Demonstrate how to create tree trunks by painting cornhusks with brown paint and printing them onto the green paper.

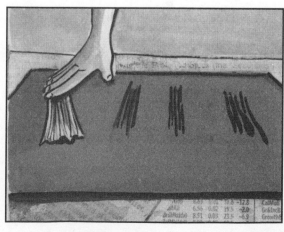

3 Show children how to create colorful foliage by dipping a bunched-up plastic bag into tempera paint and printing it onto the green paper background.

4 Use a separate plastic bag for each color. Colors will mix as they are printed on the paper background.

5 Allow prints to dry thoroughly.

6 Display prints to create an autumn wooded wonderland!

BOOK LINKS

Why Do Leaves Change Color?
by Betsy Maestro
(HarperTrophy, 1994)
An informative concept book explaining what happens to leaves in fall as they change colors and then separate from the tree.

Autumn Leaves
by Ken Robbins
(Scholastic, 1998)
This beautiful book shows full-color photos against clean white backgrounds, introducing children to many autumn leaves. A good guide for outdoor expeditions.

Harvest Cornhusk Weavings

Combine recycled materials to weave an attractive minimat or trivet. Or, join the class weavings quilt-style for a banquet mat, then spread out some autumn bounty!

Materials

- Brown paper grocery bags (enough for each child to have one 7" square)
- Cornhusks (ask families to put aside husks to dry at home after shucking), about 10 per child
- Glue
- Scissors

Setup

Precut squares from paper bags for each child. Separate dried cornhusks into strips approximately ½" long.

1 Children can work individually. Provide each child with a brown paper bag square, cornhusk strips, scissors, and glue.

2 Demonstrate how to fold the square in half, bringing the sides together, and crease down the center.

3 Show children how to make slits about ½–1" apart across the folded edge, stopping approximately ½" from the edges.

4 Have children unfold the square and spread it flat.

5 Demonstrate how to weave through the slits by slipping a cornhusk strip over and under, over and under, all the way across. (Children should begin the second cornhusk strip under if the last was started over, and continue to alternate each row.) Continue weaving cornhusk strips until the square has been filled. Have children push the cornhusk strips close together as they work.

6 Show children how to glue the ends of the cornhusk strips to the paper bag. Leave to dry.

7 Top off each harvest minimat with a big juicy apple or bake some of these pumpkin muffins together! (Check for food allergies first).

Pumpkin Muffins

(Makes 12)

12 muffin papers
1 cup canned pumpkin
2 ripe bananas
1 cup milk
2 tablespoon brown sugar
1 teaspoon ground cinnamon
1 teaspoon ground nutmeg
½ teaspoon salt
2 large eggs
½ cup raisins, sweetened dried cranberries,
    or chopped nuts (optional)

1 Preheat oven to 300°F. Place muffin papers in muffin tins.

2 Combine all ingredients and mix until smooth. Stir in raisins, cranberries, or nuts, if desired. Spoon the mixture into the paper muffin cups. Bake for 45 minutes.

3 Remove muffins from tin. When cool enough to handle, place muffins on the cornhusk mats.

BOOK LINKS

The Autumn Equinox: Celebrating the Harvest
by Ellen B. Jackson
(Millbrook Press Trade, 2000)
Explores the history of the autumn equinox and ancient celebrations of the harvest. Includes an adaptation of a Native American legend and an assortment of classroom projects and recipes.

Corn Is Maize: The Gift of the Indians
by Aliki
(HarperTrophy, 1986)
Popcorn, corn on the cob, cornbread, corncob pipes, tacos, tamales, tortillas, and many other good things come from this plant. Here's the story of how Indian farmers thousands of years ago found and nourished this wild grass plant, and how they shared this knowledge with European settlers.

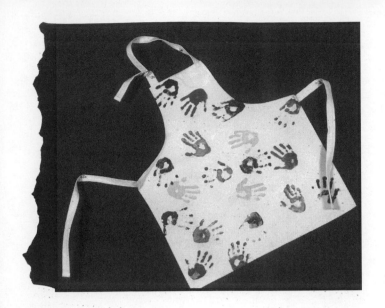

Helping Hand Apron

This "hand" printed apron makes a great collaborative class gift. It's also a fun way to teach color mixing!

Materials

- Newspaper (to cover tables)
- Apron (sold in kitchen supply or art stores; a solid light background is preferable)
- Textile paint (in primary colors)
- Paintbrushes
- 6 shallow containers

1 Have a class discussion about how children help out at home. What are some ways we use our hands to help?

2 Divide the class into partners.

3 The workstation should be large enough to spread out an apron and the trays of textile ink. Cover work surfaces with newspaper. Provide each station with trays of primary color textile ink, three extra trays for color mixing, and six brushes.

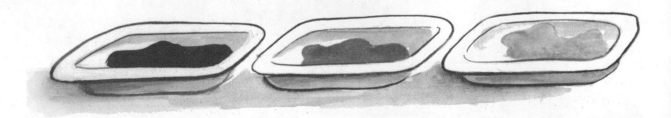

4 Demonstrate color mixing. What happens when yellow is mixed with blue? Have partners use one brush for each color, adding yellow onto one half of a clean tray with the yellow brush, and blue onto the other half of the tray with the blue brush. Taking a new, clean brush, have partners mix the colors, coating this brush with the newly mixed color. Have partners mix the other colors for new combinations.

5 Demonstrate how one partner can paint the other's palm and fingers with textile paint. They then press the painted hand onto the flat apron, leaving a handprint.

6 Have the other partner paint a different color onto the first child's palm and fingers. Each child can make one or two handprints on the apron. When the apron has been printed as desired, set aside to dry.

7 When textile inks are dry, they can be heat-set by ironing the reverse side of the apron. This will prevent the colors from washing out or bleeding.

8 Present the apron as a class gift—perhaps to someone who helps in the classroom.

BOOK LINKS

Ma Dear's Aprons
by Pat McKissack
(Atheneum, 1997)
This affectionate tale tells the story of a week in the life of a turn-of-the-century boy and his mother.

The Color Kittens
by Margaret Wise Brown
(Golden Books, 2000)
In this classic first book about colors, kittens mix paints to create every color in the world!

Little Blue and Little Yellow
by Leo Lionni
(Mulberry Books, 1995)
This is a clever story of two colors and their friendship. A great introduction to blending colors!

Color Dance
by Ann Jonas
(Greenwillow, 1989)
Using the device of a graceful scarf dance, the author introduces young readers to the concept of color combinations.

Spaghetti Place Mats

Use this project to introduce a study of lines. Choose special colors for a seasonal or holiday place mat.

Materials

- Newspaper (to cover tables)
- Fabric or craft foam (12" x 18" rectangles), one per child
- Textile inks in different colors
- Shallow containers
- Precut strings (8–10" lengths) with a large bead threaded and tied on one end of each, one per child

1 Discuss lines with your class. Ask children to describe the difference between straight and curvy lines. Who has eaten spaghetti? What does spaghetti look like before it's been cooked? What kind of line is that? What does spaghetti look like after it's been cooked? What kind of line is that?

2 Divide the class into groups. Cover work surfaces with newspaper. Provide each group with shallow containers of textile inks, strings, and fabric or foam place mats.

3 Show children how to hold the bead on the string and dip it into the textile paint. Gently press the string into the paint to coat it with color. Use a separate piece of string for each color of paint.

4 Holding onto the bead, children can lift the string from the paint and place it on the place mat, allowing it to curve and twist naturally.

5 Show children how to press firmly with fingertips along the string's path, making a print on the place mat.

6 Have children lift the string off and put it aside.

7 Let children repeat the process again and again, using a new string for each color until the desired effect is reached.

8 Allow paints to dry completely on the place mats. To set the paint, iron the back side of the fabric printed mats. For craft foam place mats, iron the top side, first placing a clean sheet of newsprint over the printed surface to protect the iron.

BOOK LINKS

The Straight Line Wonder
by Mem Fox
(Mondo, 1997)
Three straight lines are best friends. But when one of them gets tired of being straight all of the time, his friends are embarrassed and leave him by himself. What follows teaches the value of being true to oneself.

Weather Mobiles

Children will enjoy creating their own moving weather patterns. This sculpture project explores the concept of 3-D as kids learn about the seasons.

Materials

- Pencils
- Scissors
- Glue
- White or blue pipe cleaners
- Clear tape
- Hole punch

SUN

- 6" yellow posterboard circles, 2 per child

CLOUD

- Precut posterboard cloud (similar size as sun), one per child
- Cotton (cotton balls or jewelry box liners), one handful per child

RAIN

- Blue plastic straw, one per child

SNOWFLAKES

- 3" square of white paper, one per child
- 4" square of white paper, one per child

SKY

- Blue plastic plate, one per child

Setup

For each child:

- Precut a blue plastic plate. Cut off the outer rim; then follow a spiral cutting pattern.
- Precut pipe cleaners in different lengths.
- You might provide children each with a large self-sealing bag labeled with their name in which to store their parts over the course of the project.

NOTE: Depending on children's age, do this project over two or three days.

Sun

1 Children can work individually. Provide each child with 2 yellow posterboard circles, pencils, and scissors.

2 Demonstrate how children can make a sun from the yellow posterboard circles. Ask them to locate the center of each circle and make a dot with their pencils. Using the scissors, have them cut into the circle, stopping at the dot. Then they repeat with the other circle.

3 Show children how to fit the two circles together by crossing the slits and pushing them toward the center dots.

4 Have children take the circles apart and cut triangle notches along each edge, making sunrays.

5 Recombine the two circles as before to make a sun!

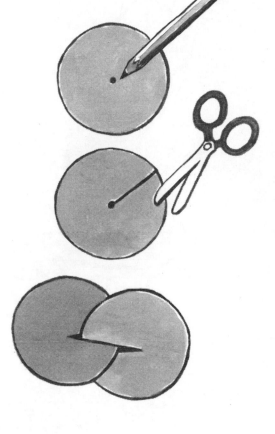

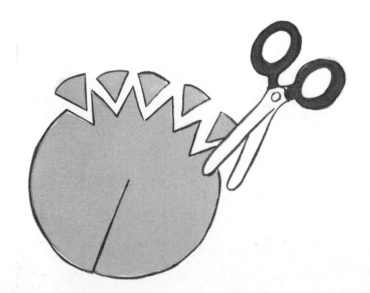

Clouds and Rain

1 Provide each child with a precut cloud, cotton, glue, and a blue plastic straw.

2 Show children how to stretch the cotton to cover the cloud template.

3 Demonstrate gluing and positioning the cotton.

4 Repeat this process with the reverse side of the cloud. Let dry.

5 Have children cut the straw into three or four pieces to make raindrops.

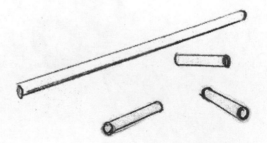

Snow

1 Provide each child with 3" and 4" squares of white paper and scissors.

2 Have children begin with one square, folding the paper diagonally and matching the opposite corners. Then they press the crease down, fold again, and press the crease down once more.

3 Demonstrate how to cut through all the folds or along the outer edges, notching slits and shapes. Children should not cut completely across the folded paper.

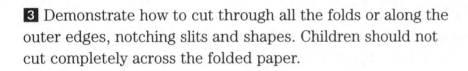

4 Have children open up the folds and flatten out the snowflake.

5 Let children repeat folding and cutting with the other piece of paper, making different designs. Then they can open and flatten their snowflakes.

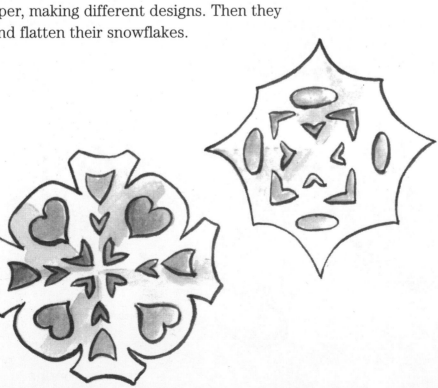

To assemble

1 Have an adult (aide or parent volunteer) work with each child individually. Gather the children's sun, clouds, rain, snow, spiral-cut paper plates, scissors, pipe cleaners, clear tape, and a hole punch.

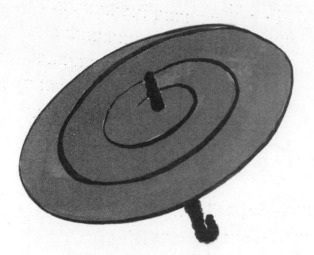

2 Using the hole punch, the adult can create a hole in the center of the spiral-cut plate. Have the child work from below the plate and push a pipe cleaner up through the hole. The adult can help fold the pipe cleaner to create a knot, then secure the knot below the plate with clear tape.

3 It will be easier to balance the mobile if the weather components can hang freely as they are assembled. Suspend the spiral-cut plate by attaching the top of the pipe cleaner to something overhead. (Try stretching a string across the room. Hang the mobiles from this line. To make mobiles reachable for little helping hands, you can temporarily hang coat hangers, then dangle the mobiles from these.)

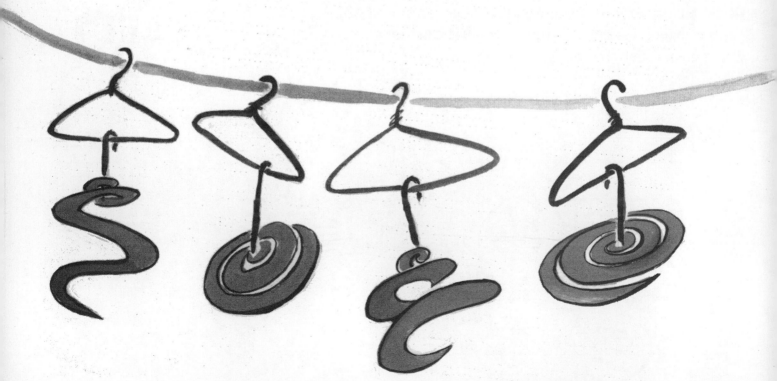

(project continued on page 33)

Movable Me, Pages 6–11

ABOVE: **Family Portraits,** Pages 12–15

BELOW: **My Home,** Pages 16–18

ABOVE: **Autumn Tree Prints,** Pages 19–20

BELOW: **Harvest Cornhusk Weavings,** Pages 21–23

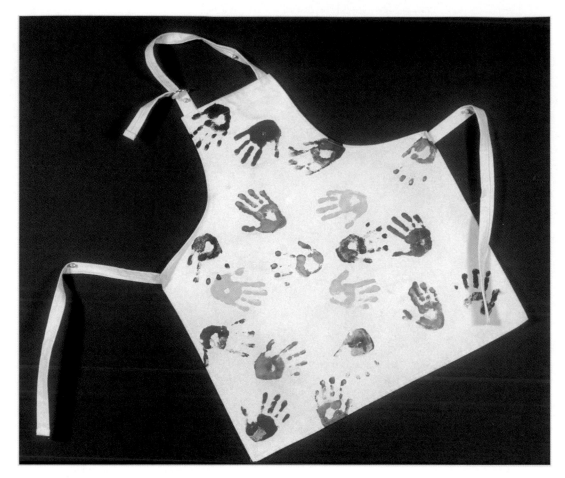

ABOVE: **Helping Hand Apron,** Pages 24–25

BELOW: **Spaghetti Place Mats,** Pages 26–27

RIGHT: **Weather Mobiles,** Pages 28–34

BELOW: **Chinese New Year Dragon Puppets,** Pages 35–40

ABOVE: **Egg Carton Flowers,** Pages 50–52

BELOW: **Craft Foam Visors,** Pages 53–55

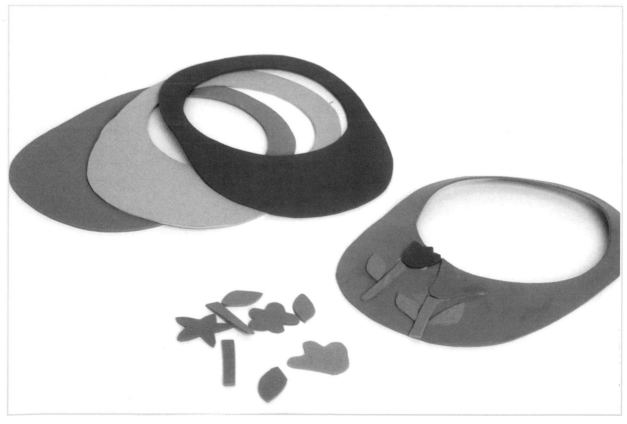

ABOVE: **Origami Oceans,** Pages 56–57

BELOW: **Butterfly Masks,** Pages 58–60

4 Punch a hole at the top of one section of the sun. Have children push a pipe cleaner through the top center of the assembled sun. Punch a second hole in the center section of the spiral-cut plate. Starting from below, have the student push the pipe cleaner up through the center of the spiral, allowing the sun to dangle approximately 3 inches below. Pull through, fold to make a knot, and secure with clear tape.

5 Continue attaching weather elements each time, moving farther out from the center of the spiral. Punch a hole in the center top of the cloud. Pull a pipe cleaner through, fold to make a knot, and secure the knot with the clear tape. Then, about halfway down the blue spiral, punch another hole and attach the cloud.

6 Move halfway down the remaining portion of the spiral and punch another hole. Attach the snow, first punching a hole through the top of the snowflake, attaching a pipe cleaner, then suspending the snowflake from the spiral. Move farther down the spiral, punch a hole, and repeat the process to dangle a second snowflake at a different length.

7 At the end of the spiral punch several holes to attach the individual straw raindrops. Push a pipe cleaner through each straw section. Fold the pipe cleaner to form a knot below each straw. Suspend each raindrop at a different length, pushing the pipe cleaners up through the holes punched in the spiral, folding the pipe cleaners to create knots, and securing with clear tape.

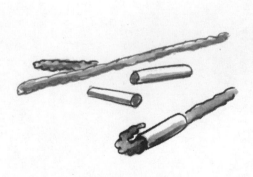

Chinese New Year Dragon Puppets

Welcome the Lunar Year with
a Chinese Dragon parade.
Children transform egg cartons,
a paper bag, and odds 'n' ends
to make simple puppets.

Materials

FOR EACH CHILD:

- Spiky dragon scales cut from the center divider of a cardboard egg carton
- 2 individual egg sections for dragon eyes (cut from a cardboard egg carton)
- Mouth and teeth patterns (copy page 39 onto white paper)
- 2 red construction paper horns and one tongue (see page 40 for size guide)
- 2 large wiggle eyes
- Red paper party bags (available in card and party stores)
- 2 white craft feathers
- Black crayon

FOR EACH GROUP:

- Newspaper (to cover tables)
- Scissors
- Red tempera paint
- Paintbrushes
- Containers for paint
- Stapler
- Glue

DAY ONE

1 Divide the class into groups. Cover work surfaces with newspaper. Provide each group with red tempera, paintbrushes, and containers for paint. Provide each child with egg carton dragon scales and two egg carton eyes.

2 Have children paint the dragon scales and dragon eyes red. Leave to dry.

DAY TWO

1 Provide children with precut mouths and teeth, tongues, horns, their painted scales and eyes, scissors, wiggle eyes, a stapler, and glue.

2 Show children how to create the dragon's mouth. First have them use crayon to color one side of the mouth black.

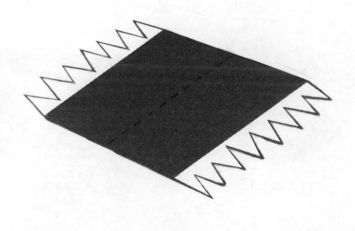

3 Demonstrate how to fold the dragon's top and bottom teeth inward. Then fold the dragon's mouth in half the short way.

4 Have an adult helper work with children individually to make curly tongues. Demonstrate how to curl the red construction paper tongue, beginning with the narrow end and wrapping the paper around a pencil. Remove from the pencil and allow the curl to loosen.

5 Have children attach the curled tongue inside the mouth with glue.

6 Help children attach a white craft feather below the bottom set of teeth by stapling the feather below the black paper.

7 Show children how to glue the completed mouth under the fold of the paper bag.

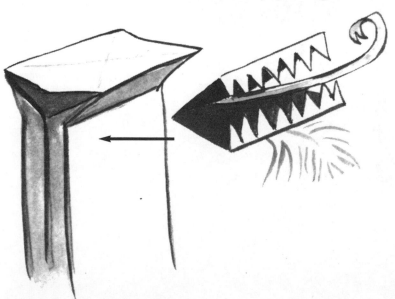

BOOK LINKS

Celebrating Chinese New Year
by Diane Hoyt-Goldsmith
(Holiday House, 1999)
A Chinese-American boy and his
family prepare for the coming Chinese
New Year. Introduces the holiday's
foods and customs and provides
information about the history of
San Francisco's Chinatown.

Lunar New Year for Kids: A Hands-on Workbook for Parents and Teachers
by Cindy Roberts
(Cindy Roberts, 2000)
This classroom resource includes
many new ways of celebrating
the Lunar New Year.

The Dancing Dragon
by Marcia K. Vaughan
(Mondo, 1996)
A great read-aloud book with
an accordion style pull-out
dancing dragon. Good lead into
a class parade!

Moonbeams, Dumplings & Dragon Boats: A Treasury of Chinese Holiday Tales, Activities, and Recipes
by Nina Simonds and Leslie Swartz
(Gulliver Books, 2002)
This book is filled with recipes,
hands-on family activities, and
traditional tales to read aloud and
inspire celebration of all the
lunar holidays.

8 Have an adult helper help staple the egg carton scales to the back of the bag. Attach the scales at the base and the top of the paper bag. Then staple each horn onto a top outside corner of the bag. Staple the dragon eyes below the horns. Finally, staple white feathers behind the eyes at the sides of the bag.

9 Have children glue wiggle eyes onto the red egg carton eyes. Leave to dry.

10 Have your own dragon parade with the completed puppets!

Chinese New Year Dragon Puppet Patterns

mouth and teeth

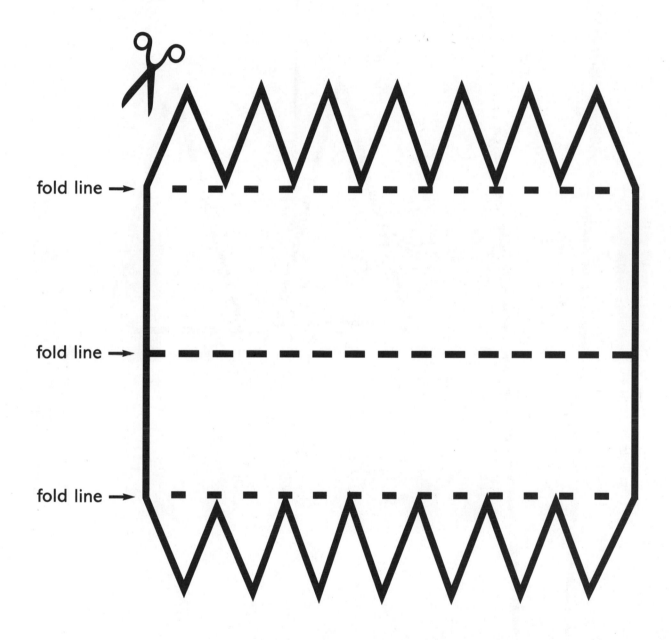

fold line →

fold line →

fold line →

Chinese New Year
Dragon Puppet Patterns

tongue

horns

Recycled School Buses

Children make their own bus from recycled materials— and include their friends on board!

Materials

DAY ONE

FOR EACH GROUP:
- Newspaper (to cover tables)
- Yellow tempera paint
- Paintbrushes
- Shallow containers for paint

FOR EACH CHILD:
- Copy of page 45
- Shoebox without lid (or comparable sized box)
- Tea (or comparable sized) box

DAY TWO

FOR EACH GROUP:
- Stapler
- Glue
- Scissors

FOR EACH CHILD:
- Black construction paper bus stripes (see size guides on page 46)
- 2 red construction paper brake lights (see size guides on page 46)
- 4 plastic yogurt (or comparable sized) lids
- 4 black construction paper wheels (see size guides on page 46)

DAY THREE

FOR EACH GROUP:
- Markers and/or crayons for drawing passengers

FOR EACH CHILD:
- White construction paper for front, back, and side windows (see size guides on page 46)

DAY FOUR

- Recycled clear plastic berry or fruit containers for the front windows
- 4 brads per child
- 2 plastic water or soda bottle tops for front lights
- Aluminum foil for bumpers
- Scissors
- Glue

DAY ONE

1 Discuss what children know about school buses. Distribute page 45 and have children write their names and color in the bus. Read and discuss the safety rules together.

2 Divide the class into groups. Cover work surfaces with newspaper. Provide each group with boxes, yellow tempera, paintbrushes, and containers for paint.

3 Have each child paint all sides of a shoebox and a tea box with yellow tempera. Leave to dry overnight.

DAY TWO

1 Help children staple the smaller box to the larger box, forming the front of the bus.

2 Provide each group with black construction paper bus stripes, red construction paper brake lights, plastic yogurt lids, black construction paper wheels, scissors, and glue.

3 Help children glue the black construction paper stripes to the sides and back of the larger yellow box, then position and glue the red brake lights on the back of the bus below the stripes.

4 Have children glue a black construction paper wheel inside each of four plastic yogurt lids. Set aside.

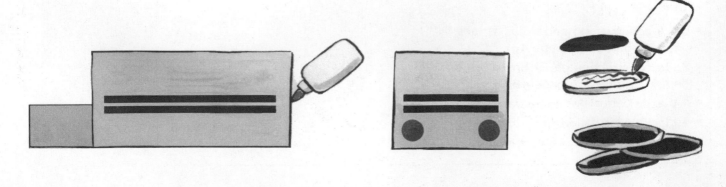

DAY THREE

1 Who rides the school bus? Who drives the school bus? Have children sing "The Wheels on the Bus" (see words on page 47).

2 Provide children with white construction paper bus windows, markers, and/or crayons.

3 Encourage children to draw a bus driver and passengers, one per square, and glue them onto the bus.

DAY FOUR

Setup

Poke holes through the center of each plastic lid wheel, and through matching front and back holes on each side of the bus, about ½" up from the bottom of the box. Cut the base or top of a recycled clear plastic fruit container in half to form the bus front window.

1 Provide each child with his or her bus, wheels, window drawings, 2 plastic water bottle tops, aluminum foil, clear plastic front window, 4 brads, scissors, and glue. Have children glue their window drawings in position.

2 Demonstrate how to fold the foil and position it to create a bumper.

3 Show children how to position and glue the headlights and front window.

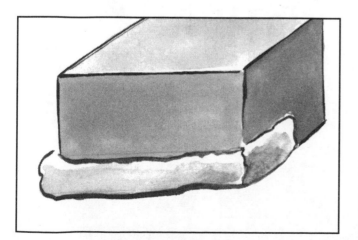 

4 Demonstrate how to attach the wheels using the brads.
An adult helper (aide or parent volunteer) should circulate
to help individuals assemble their bus elements.

SCHOOL BUS RULES

Here's how to stay safe on the bus!

1. Stay sitting down.
2. Keep your hands and arms inside the bus.
3. Speak quietly so the driver can concentrate.
4. Be kind to your fellow passengers. Keep your hands to yourself.
5. Do not eat, drink, or litter.

YIELD

STOP

SPEED LIMIT 25

_____'s School Bus

Recycled School Bus Patterns

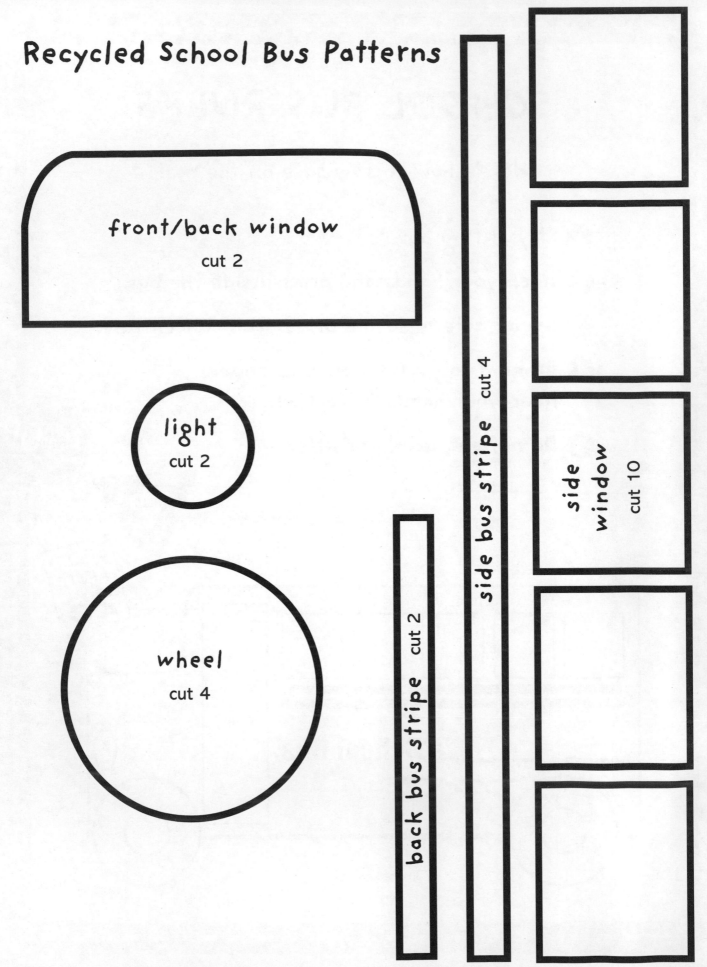

front/back window
cut 2

light
cut 2

wheel
cut 4

back bus stripe cut 2

side bus stripe cut 4

side window cut 10

THE WHEELS ON THE BUS

The wheels on the bus go round and round;
round and round;
round and round.
The wheels on the bus go round and round,
all through the town!

The horn on the bus goes beep, beep, beep;
beep, beep beep;
beep, beep, beep.
The horn on the bus goes beep, beep, beep,
all through the town!

The wipers on the bus go swish, swish, swish;
swish, swish, swish;
swish, swish, swish.
The wipers on the bus go swish, swish, swish,
all through the town!

The people on the bus go up and down;
up and down;
up and down.
The people on the bus go up and down,
all through the town!

The babies on the bus go waa, waa, waa;
waa, waa, waa;
waa, waa, waa.
The babies on the bus go waa, waa, waa,
all through the town!

The parents on the bus go shh, shh, shh;
shh, shh, shh;
shh, shh, shh.
The parents on the bus go shh, shh, shh,
all through the town!

Valentine Splatter

Jackson Pollock meets St. Valentine!
This fun card combines cutting,
stenciling, and abstract expressionism.
The card folds to make its own
envelope, and the stencil leaves
room for a Valentine message.

Materials

- Newspaper (to cover tables)
- 6" x 9" white or pink construction paper (cut 9" x 12" sheets in half), one sheet per child
- Contact paper or any other low-tack, sticky-back paper, cut into 3½" squares, one sheet per child
- Scissors
- Tempera paints in red and pink
- Containers for paint
- Water container
- Old, sterilized toothbrushes

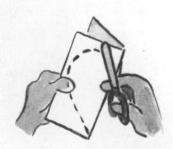

1 Divide the class into small groups. Cover work areas with newspaper. Provide each group with construction paper, contact paper squares, scissors, tempera paints, water in containers, and old toothbrushes.

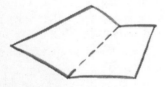

2 Demonstrate how to fold the contact paper square in half and cut out half of a heart. Then unfold the contact paper to reveal a heart!

3 Show children how to peel off the backing from the sticky paper heart, then stick the heart onto the construction paper in the desired spot.

4 Demonstrate splatter painting, first dipping a toothbrush into the water container, then into a paint container. Brush the thumb across the surface of the paint-loaded brush, aiming the splatter over the construction paper card. The paint will not soak into the contact paper heart.

5 Have children repeat this process with each of the paint colors until they achieve the desired effect.

6 Have children remove the sticky heart and reuse it on more cards. Allow the cards to dry.

7 Help children write a name or message in the heart.

8 Fold cards in half to create an envelope. Seal the card with a sticker, tape or glue.

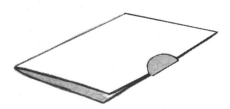

BOOK LINKS

It's Valentine's Day
by Jack Prelutsky
(Econo-Clad Books, 1999)
This book has simple and easy-to-read Valentine's Day poems for kids of all ages.

Somebody Loves You, Mr. Hatch
by Eileen Spinelli
(Aladdin Paperbacks, 1996)
When a big valentine filled with candy is delivered from a secret admirer, Mr. Hatch views everyone as a potential friend and becomes a changed person.

Jackson Pollock
by Mike Venezia
(Children's Press, 1994)
The author combines words, comics, and paintings for a fun exploration of the work of Jackson Pollock.

Egg Carton Flowers

Create colorful flower bouquets in your classroom from recycled egg cartons.

Materials

- Newspaper (to cover tables)
- Recycled toilet paper rolls, one per child
- 4" cardboard circle base, one per child
- Recycled cardboard egg cartons, with egg sections cut apart into petals (see photo above left), 12 sections per child
- Green pipe cleaners (about 12 per child)
- "Gift card" (copy page 52 onto white paper and cut apart), one per child
- Glue
- Tempera paints in assorted colors
- Paint containers
- Paintbrushes
- Pencils
- Clear tape

DAY ONE

1 Divide the class into small groups. Cover tables with newspaper. Provide each group with paper rolls, cardboard circle bases, precut egg carton flowers, glue, tempera paint, paint containers, and brushes.

2 Show children how to center and glue the paper roll to the cardboard base. This creates the structure for the vase. Let dry.

3 Have children paint their flowers various colors.

4 Once the glue has set, children can paint the vases and bases with tempera. Let dry.

DAY TWO

1 Cover tables with newspaper. Provide children with their painted egg carton flowers, vases, and pipe cleaners.

2 With a pencil, poke a hole at the base of each flower. Demonstrate how to thread a pipe cleaner through, starting from below the hole and aiming up into the flower.

3 Help them bend the pipe cleaner at the top to keep it from slipping back through the hole.

4 Repeat this process with all the flowers. Help children arrange the flowers in a bouquet in the vase.

5 Invite children to complete a gift card and tape it to their vase!

BOOK LINKS

Flower Garden
by Eve Bunting
(Harcourt, 1999)
This beautiful book describes a close, loving family who plants a garden in a city flowerbox.

Bumblebee, Bumblebee, Do You Know Me?: A Garden Guessing Game
by Anne F. Rockwell
(HarperCollins, 1999)
This garden book is full of the scents, textures, colors, and shapes of flowers. Features pairings of bright silk-screen illustrations with simple riddles.

The Tiny Seed
by Eric Carle
(Simon & Schuster, 1990)
Collage illustrations and simple text follow the adventures of a tiny seed.

Gift Card Patterns

I Love You!

From,

_____

For my friend

_____

From,

_____

TO _____

I made these for you!

LOVE, _____

Dear _____

Get well soon!

Love, _____

To _____

Thanks for

_____

From,

_____

I MISS YOU!

Love, _____

Craft Foam Visors

Here's a spring hat project for everyone— it's also a great way for kids to protect their face and eyes from the bright sun!

Materials
- Precut craft foam visors in assorted colors (use pattern on page 55 as a size guide), one per child
- Precut craft foam shapes (enough so that children have a choice of flowers, leaves, stems, bugs, snakes, animals, birds, dinosaurs, or any other shapes)
- Scrap craft foam in assorted colors
- Scissors
- Glue

1 Discuss sun safety with your class. Ask children to share ideas about how to keep the sun off their faces.

2 Divide the class into small groups. Provide each group with an assortment of precut foam visors, precut shapes, scraps, scissors, and glue.

Twelve Hats for Lena:
A Book of Months
by Karen Katz
(Margaret McElderry, 2002)
A hat project for every month of
the year!

Caps for Sale: A Tale of a
Peddler, Some Monkeys and
Their Monkey Business
by Esphyr Slobodkina
(HarperCollins, 1985)
This is a simple, silly story of a
peddler who sells caps from a tall,
tottering pile on his head. The
book is full of repetitive rhythm
that 3- and 4-year-olds will adore.

A Three Hat Day
by Laura Geringer
(HarperCollins, 1987)
A hat collector has a terrible day
until he meets his true love in the
hat section of the department store.

3 Demonstrate how children can cut their own shapes or use precut shapes to decorate their visor. Show them how to glue the pieces to the visor. Encourage experimentation!

4 Have a class parade or arrange a class portrait with everyone wearing their new visor!

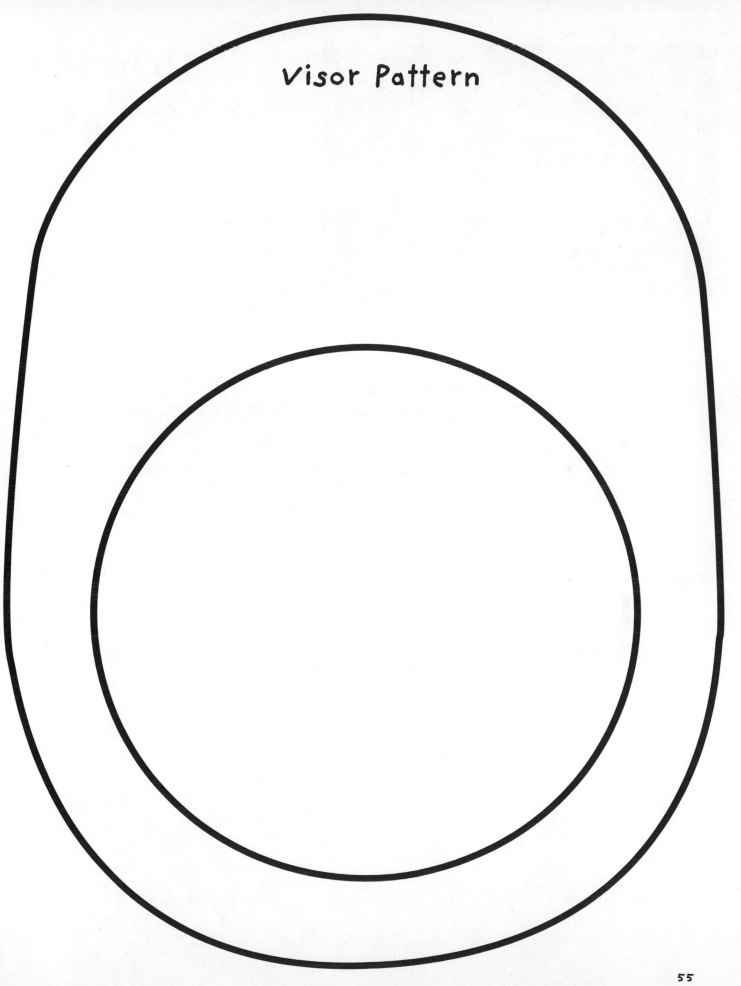

Visor Pattern

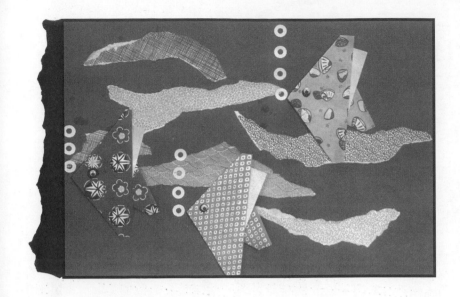

Origami Oceans

Here's an easy introduction to traditional paper folding. It's also a great study of pattern and a tie-in to ocean studies.

Materials

- Patterned origami paper or 6" squares of colored paper, 3 sheets per child
- 12" x 18" blue construction paper, one sheet per child
- Recycled business envelopes with blue patterned linings, several per child
- Wiggle eyes, 3 per child
- Glue
- Self-adhesive or sticky-backed white hole reinforcements, about 10 per child

1 Divide the class into small groups. Provide each group with origami or colored paper, blue construction paper, envelopes, glue, and hole reinforcements.

2 Demonstrate how to fold a simple origami fish. Make a diagonal fold beginning slightly below the upper left corner, and finishing slightly above the bottom right corner. Crease the paper upward.

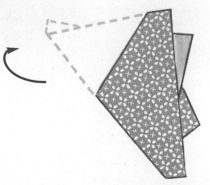

3 Fold the left side of the new shape behind and downward to create the shape shown. The two small triangles form the fish's tail.

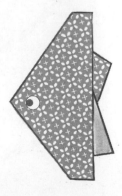

4 Encourage children to repeat the folding pattern with more squares to create more fish.

5 Show children how to tear strips of the envelope liners to simulate water, gluing these strips into the desired positions on the blue construction paper.

6 Have children arrange the fish in their ocean and glue into the desired position.

7 Demonstrate how to position and glue wiggle eyes on the fish.

8 Show children how to make air bubbles by placing hole reinforcements rising from fish mouths.

BOOK LINKS

The Complete Book of Origami: Step-by-Step Instructions in Over 1000 Diagrams
by Robert J. Lang
(Dover, 1989)
This is a resource guide for teachers with loads of inspiration and easy directions.

Look Inside the Ocean
by Laura Crema
(Grosset & Dunlap, 1998)
This colorfully illustrated book is full of information about the different areas of the ocean and creatures living there.

The Underwater Alphabet Book
by Jerry Pallotta
(Charlesbridge Publishing, 1991)
From angelfish to zebra pipefish, an alphabet of tropical creatures leads readers through this ecological system. Includes colorful illustrations and fact-filled text about the fascinating life on the coral reef.

Fish Eyes: A Book You Can Count On
by Lois Ehlert
(Harcourt, 1990)
Rhyming text lets children view underwater life through fish eyes. Vivid fish swim through the book, one reappearing to guide the counting fun.

Butterfly Masks

Kids will love transforming into butterflies with these colorful collage masks. Choreograph a migration dance with your class of beautiful butterflies.

Materials

- Newspaper (to cover tables)
- Precut tagboard butterfly masks (copy page 60 onto heavy cardstock and cut along lines), one per child
- Craft tissue paper in an assortment of colors
- Glue/water mixture (about half glue and half water)
- Shallow containers for the glue mixture
- Paintbrushes
- 12" ribbons, 2 per child
- Glue

1 Divide the class into small groups. Cover each work area with newspaper. Provide each group with precut masks, tissue paper, shallow containers with the diluted glue mixture, paintbrushes, ribbons, and glue.

2 Demonstrate how children can tear pieces of tissue paper, paint the mask with the diluted glue, and position the pieces on the mask. Encourage children to experiment with different colors as they design their butterflies. Let masks dry.

3 Flip masks to the reverse side and position the ribbons near the outer eye area. Glue ribbons into position. Let dry.

4 Tie on the finished masks and have a migration dance!

BOOK LINKS

The Journey of a Butterfly
by Carolyn Scrace
(Franklin Watts, 2000)
Describes the life cycle and annual migration of the monarch butterfly.

From Caterpillar to Butterfly
by Deborah Heiligman
(HarperTrophy, 1996)
A class watches a caterpillar each day as it grows and changes. Soon, it disappears into a hard shell called a chrysalis. Then the chrysalis breaks, and a beautiful butterfly flies out of the jar! A perfect beginner's guide to the mystery of metamorphosis.

Monarch Butterfly
by Gail Gibbons
(Holiday House, 1991)
This book describes the life cycle, body parts, and behavior of the monarch butterfly.

Butterfly Mask Pattern

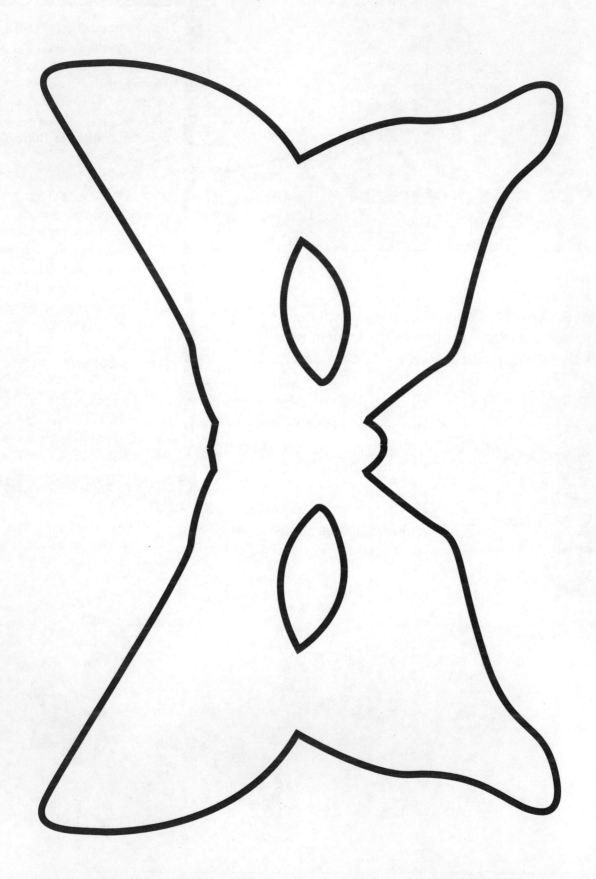

Dear Families,

We have many fun art projects planned this year. Please help us gather materials by saving the following items at home and bringing them to our classroom. Encourage creative recycling!

- Cardboard egg and milk cartons
- Shoe, tea, and cereal boxes
- Cardboard pieces
- Fabric scraps
- Paper grocery bags
- Cornhusks (saved and dried after shucking)
- Plastic bags
- String
- Cotton balls or jewelry box liners
- Lunch bags
- Used, sterilized toothbrushes
- Business envelopes with patterned linings
- Used manila folders
- Yogurt lids
- Plastic bottle caps
- Aluminum foil
- Clear, plastic food containers

Also, please feel free to join us in the classroom and help with our art projects. We have many opportunities for adult helpers!

Sincerely,

Additional Resources

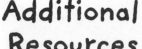

Alphabet Art: With A–Z Animal Art & Fingerplays
by Judy Press
(Williamson Publishing, 1997)

The Art of Teaching Art to Children: In School and at Home
by Nancy Beal and Gloria Bley Miller
(Farrar, Straus, & Giroux, 2001)

Art for the Very Young: Ages 3-6
by Kelly Elizabeth and Joanne McConville
(Instructional Fair, 1998)

The Big Messy but Easy to Clean Up Art Book
by MaryAnn F. Kohl
(Gryphon House, 2000)

Child's Play: 200 Instant Crafts and Activities for Preschoolers
by Leslie Hamilton
(Crown Publishing Group, 1989)

Discovering Great Artists: Hands-on Art for Children in the Styles of the Great Masters
by MaryAnn F. Kohl
(Bright Ring, 1997)

Doing Art Together
by M. Muriel Silberstein-Storfer
(Harry N. Abrams, 1997)

Ecoart!: Earth-Friendly Art and Craft Experiences for 3- to 9-Year-Olds
by Laurie Carlson
(Williamson Publishing, 1992)

Everyday Art for Kids: Projects to Unlock Creativity
by Carolyn Holm
(Mockingbird, 1996)

First Art: Art Experiences for Toddlers and Twos
by MaryAnn F. Kohl, Renee F. Ramsey, Dana Bowman, and Katheryn Davis
(Gryphon House, 2002)

Kids Create!: Art & Craft Experiences for 3- to 9-Year-Olds
by Laurie Carlson
(Williamson Publishing, 2003)

The Little Hands Art Book/Exploring Arts & Crafts With 2- to 6-Year-Olds
by Judy Press
(Williamson Publishing, 2003)

Math Play!
by Diane McGowan and Mark Schrooten
(Williamson Publishing, 1997)

Mudworks: Creative Clay, Dough, and Modeling Experiences
by MaryAnn F. Kohl
(Bright Ring, 1992)

My Animal Art Class
by Nellie Shepherd
(DK Publishing, 2003)

My Art Class
by Nellie Shepherd
(DK Publishing, 2003)

My Picture Art Class
by Nellie Shepherd
(DK Publishing, 2003)

My Puppet Art Class
by Nellie Shepherd
(DK Publishing, 2003)

Preschool Art: It's the Process, Not the Product
by MaryAnn F. Kohl
(Gryphon House, 1994)

Science Arts: Discovering Science Through Art Experiences
by Jean Potter and MaryAnn F. Kohl
(Bright Ring, 1993)

Scribble Art: Independent Creative Art Experiences for Children
by MaryAnn F. Kohl
(Bright Ring, 1994)

Teaching Art With Books Kids Love: Teaching Art Appreciation, Elements of Art, and Principles of Design With Award-winning Children's Books
by Darcie Clark Frohardt
(Fulcrum, 1999)

Using Art to Make Art
by Wendy M. L. Libby
(Delmar Learning, 2000)

365 Days of Creative Play: For Children 2 Years & Up
by Sheila Ellison, Judith Gray, and Susan Ferdinandi
(Sourcebooks Trade, 1995)

Web Sites

Explore these Web sites for additional inspiration and project ideas! Web site addresses and information may have changed since this book was published. Please check the Web sites and assess their content before directing children to them.

www.sitesforteachers.com

slider-secure.vendercom.com

www.kinderart.com

www.perpetualpreschool.com

www.123child.com

www.edu-orchard.net

www.crayola.com

www.lessonplanz.com

www.thematicunit.com

www.teacherszone.com

www.edhelper.com

www.everythingpreschool.com